with the Banana Slug String Band

*Dedicated to my Mother Sharla who taught me to dance with life's music
and how to sense the fragrance of the changing season.
This was particularly skillful since I grew up in Los Angeles.
This song was written on her 1952 Martin guitar. —SVZ*

A Sharing Nature With Children Book

Library of Congress Cataloging-in-Publication Data

Van Zandt, Steve.
  River song / by Steve Van Zandt ; illustrated by Katherine Zecca. -- 1st ed.
     p. cm.
  Summary: "A river is a wonderful thing, from the trickle of snowmelt to the ocean, and from icy winter through a warm autumn--and is celebrated in this volume through illustrations, verse and a song by a popular children's band (CD enclosed with book)"--Provided by publisher.
  ISBN 978-1-58469-093-1 (hardback) -- ISBN 978-1-58469-094-8 (pbk.) 1. Stream animals--Juvenile literature. 2. Rivers--Juvenile literature. I. Zecca, Katherine, ill. II. Title.
  QL145.V36 2007
  577.6'4--dc22
                                    2006030965

Dawn Publications

12402 Bitney Springs Road
Nevada City, CA 95959
530-274-7775
nature@dawnpub.com

Printed in China

10 9 8 7 6 5 4 3 2 1
First Edition

Design and computer production by Patty Arnold, *Menagerie Design and Publishing*

River Song

with the Banana Slug String Band

By Steve Van Zandt
with the Banana Slug String Band

Illustrated by Katherine Zecca

Dawn Publications

It happened one day on the mountain so high,
A river was born from out of the sky.
The rain and the snow came falling down
And started to run as they hit the ground.

Blurp ah pa-shoosh rumbly pound

A white rapid river makes a wonderful sound

In the short days of winter this river still flows
Under the ice and the silence of snow.
As the sun rises higher the ice it wears thin,
Like a raft it floats down as the spring thaw begins.

Blurp ah pa-shoosh rumbly pound
A white rapid river makes a wonderful sound

Over beds made of granite it sweeps and it rolls,
It is narrow and steep and so icy cold.
It carries small rocks and it grinds them to sand,
It carves out a valley and gouges the land.

Blurp ah pa-shoosh rumbly pound
A white rapid river makes a wonderful sound

It rushes along past steep canyon walls
    That echo the song of a canyon wren's call.
    Through a rainbow of flowers it bubbles and sings,
    Feeding green meadows and the new life of spring.

Blurp ah pa-shoosh rumbly pound

A white rapid river makes a wonderful sound

Over flat colored stones it riffles along,
Kingfishers and frogs join in with its songs.
With rapids and falls, spray bursting in air,
This river brings life to salmon and bear.

Blurp ah pa-shoosh rumbly pound
A white rapid river makes a wonderful sound

A strider it glides where an eddy has turned
Into dark pools in the shade of green ferns.
A dragonfly's wings shine in the sun,
While a dipper bobs by a swift rocky run.

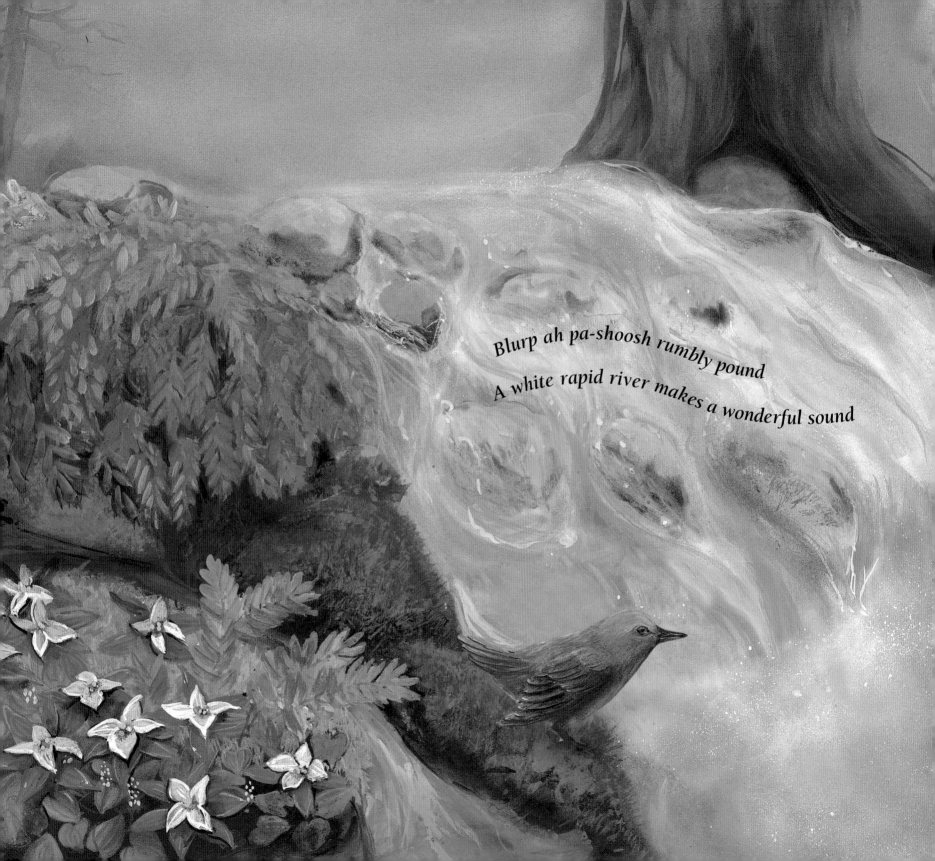

Blurp ah pa-shoosh rumbly pound

A white rapid river makes a wonderful sound

It meanders past farms and past a small town
Where on warm summer days the children come down.
They tie an old rope to the limb of a tree
And swing into the river feeling wild and free.

Blurp ah pa-shoosh rumbly pound
A white rapid river makes a wonderful sound

Their parents float in an afternoon dream
Where orange lilies cling to the side of the stream.
In the shallows the toddlers splash as they wade
While grandparents cool their feet in the shade.

Blurp ah pa-shoosh rumbly pound
A white rapid river makes a wonderful sound

Deer come to drink at the end of day's light,
In the soft muddy banks are the footprints of night.
The current divides where a small creek comes in,
Around a rock bar it's united again.

Blurp ah pa-shoosh rumbly pound
A white rapid river makes a wonderful sound

It fills up a lake and is still for a day,
But soon the wide river goes along on its way.
It rolls past rocks and banks lined with trees,
It carries small boats of fall colored leaves.

Blurp ah pa-shoosh rumbly pound
A white rapid river makes a wonderful sound

It rolls and it rolls 'til it rolls past me,
　　And it makes me smile for it's wild and free.
　　I know it is happy for it's wild and free,
　　But I wave it good bye as it enters the sea.

Blurp ah pa-shoosh rumbly pound
A white rapid river makes a wonderful sound

The water in the sea rises up to the sky
And the wind blows a cloud to the mountain so high.
The rain and the snow come falling down
And flow to the river as they hit the ground.

Blurp ah pa-shoosh rumbly pound

A white rapid river makes a wonderful sound

The Never-Ending Story of a River

River Song begins as clouds are blown to a mountain. There they cool and condense into rain or snow. Water that stays on the surface eventually trickles into a stream, which is joined by many other little streams. Eventually it becomes a river. High in the mountains, the river is narrow and steep. It moves quickly and with such force that it can tear away at the land. When it arrives at flatter lands, it widens and moves gently. In part, *River Song* is the story of the character of a river. Some of the terms used in the story describe its character. For example:

RIFFLE This is a section of a stream or river where shallow water flows swiftly over a rough rocky surface. These areas support life because the rocks provide habitat for insect larvae and the rippling water contains oxygen.

EDDY An eddy is a current of water that flows upstream. Eddies are found on the sides of the river and on the downstream side of rocks. It's fun to walk along a stream looking for eddies. You can test if it's an eddy by throwing in a small stick or leaf to see if it will float upstream.

MEANDER When a river slows down in a flat area it is likely to twist and turn like a snake, moving along in a "meander." These areas are often rich in life, because the slow moving water allows for plant growth along the banks, which in turn provides wetland habitat and food for animals.

River Song is also a story of the many forms of life that depend upon a river. Millions of plant and animal species make the river and its banks their home. This story features just a few:

CANYON WREN A small bird that lives on the rocky ledges near water. It probes its long bill into cracks in the rock to eat spiders and insects. Its call is a beautiful series of descending chirps and whistles. Most often the canyon wren is heard and not seen. This bird is the "voice" of a river canyon.

KINGFISHER The Belted Kingfisher is a bluish colored bird with a large head and a long, sharp, pointed bill. It can be seen swooping along a river as it searches for fish, frogs, crayfish, insects and reptiles to eat. It will catch fish by plunging headfirst into the water. It has a loud rattling call that can be heard all along the banks of the river.

STRIDER Water Striders are insects that live on the surface of the water. They often "skate" on calm pools along the river. They will eat any insects, living or dead, that land on the surface. Water striders have good vision and they can move very quickly without breaking through the surface of the water.

SALMON Salmon need healthy stream conditions for their survival. The best salmon streams are those with gravel beds where eggs can be laid, and calm shady pools for the safety of young salmon. They must also have plenty of vegetation on the banks to help keep the water cool and free of sediment.

BEAR Black bears that live near coastal salmon streams tend to be much larger than bears that live inland. Every year they come down to the stream and feast on the salmon as the fish swim upstream toward their spawning grounds. A healthy stream keeps the salmon swimming, which in turn keeps the bear well fed.

DRAGONFLIES Dragonflies are fierce predators. Especially during the afternoon and early evening they can be seen hovering over the water, catching mosquitoes and other insects that float in the breeze above the stream. Dragonflies are agile flyers. They can easily hover, fly backwards and quickly turn around. Their four wings beat at 20 to 30 times per second. Watch for them along the stream, as they eat their weight in insects with each meal.

DIPPER The American Dipper or Water Ouzel is a small round bird with a short stubby tail. It is often seen standing on a rock in the middle of a swiftly moving stream. The dipper has the amazing ability to walk underwater along the bottom of a stream in search of insect larvae to eat. The dipper gets it name from its habit of bobbing up and down, doing deep knee bends both in and out of the water.

TIGER LILY These orange speckled flowers grow well in moist soil. That is why they can often be seen growing over the bank of a stream.

River Song ends when the river merges with the ocean, and yet a river is a story that never ends because the water cycle really has no beginning and no ending.

Resources for More Fun and Learning

There is a wonderful abundance of resources for children and teachers about rivers, watersheds, wetlands, and much more.

River of Words: Images & Poetry in Praise of Water, Pamela Michael, ed.(2003), displays the irrepressible spirit of kids in their art and poetry about water.

ADOPT-A-WATERSHED uses place-based learning to teach about watersheds, www.adopt-a-watershed.org.

THE CENTER FOR ENVIRONMENTAL EDUCATION provides watershed resources and curriculum, and an opportunity to ask questions of EE teachers, www.ceeonline.org.

GIVE WATER A HAND encourages kids to take action within their communities involving their watersheds, www.uwex.edu/erc/gwah.

GROUNDWATER FOUNDATION has all kinds of cool stuff about groundwater for both kids and teachers, www.groundwater.org/kc/kc.html.

PROJECT WET (Water Education for Teachers) offers a wide variety of resources and programs, www.projectwet.org.

PROJECT WILD has a notable aquatic curriculum and activity guide, www.projectwild.org

RIVER OF WORDS inspires children to understand and celebrate their personal experience of a watershed through poetry and art. The website has many examples of children's art and poetry, and ROW sponsors annual contests. www.riverofwords.org.

THE WATER EDUCATION FOUNDATION is an impartial organization that offers a variety of materials and learning opportunities about water for educators and students, including Project WET. www.watereducation.org.

WOW (Wonders Of Wetlands) has publications and workshops for teachers, www.wetland.org/wowteacher.html.

River Song

Steve Van Zandt

THE BANANA SLUG STRING BAND is a group of lovable musician-educators from the coastal redwoods of Northern California. For over 20 years, this self-professed "children's ecological jam band" has excited and enlightened listeners of all ages with lessons of the Earth. With vocals, guitars, cellos, mandolin, bass, harmonica, banjo and percussion, Slug songs range from rockin' boogies to sensitive ballads. Their music, theater, puppetry and audience participation create a fun-filled learning experience. Offstage, the Slugs also develop curricula and provide workshops for teachers—showing them, for example, how to do the Water Cycle Boogie and create a rainstorm right in the classroom. The Slugs are "Airy" Larry Graff, Doug "Dirt" Greenfield, "Solar" Steve Van Zandt and "Marine" Mark Nolan. In this recording they are joined by vocalist and fiddler Laurie Lewis, "folk-cellist" Barry Phillips, and five young singers, Kayla Graff, Angelique Byard, Juanita Thomas, Grace Greenfield, and Gabby David. The Slugs can be found at www.bananaslugstringband.com.

ALTHOUGH STEVE VAN ZANDT'S MOST PUBLIC PERSONA IS AS "SOLAR," a troubadour with the Banana Slug String Band, he is a nature educator at heart. For 25 years he has been an elementary and science teacher, curriculum writer and natural science workshop presenter, and recipient of the Howard Bell Award for Outstanding Contributions to Outdoor Education. Currently he is Principal of San Mateo (California) Outdoor Education. He's a founding musician and songwriter for the Slugs, who have been touring for over 20 years—a remarkably successful record of bringing environmental awareness to children, and creative teaching techniques to teachers. Throughout, Steve has kept a foot in the water: he's a river rafting guide and avid surfer. He lives in Bonny Doon, California with his wife Laura and his teenage sons, Nathan, Colin and Skyler.

KATHERINE ZECCA loves to camp with her horse in the rugged North Cascades of the Pacific Northwest, an activity that "has allowed many intimate experiences with what nature has to give," she says. She always brings a sketch book with her, drawing the things she finds. Then she creates a larger version, and finishes it with acrylic paints and colored pencils. Although some of the illustrations are stylized, she tries to keep the flora and fauna as accurate as possible. Katherine is a graduate of the Art Institute of Seattle, and lives in Snohomish, Washington.

Other "Creative Non-Fiction" Books That Encourage Appreciation for Nature

Eliza and the Dragonfly by Susie Caldwell Rinehart, illustrated by Anisa Claire Hovemann. Almost despite herself, Eliza becomes entranced by the "awful" dragonfly nymph—and before long, both of them are transformed.

The Web at Dragonfly Pond by Brian "Fox" Ellis, illustrated by Michael S. Maydak. Fishing with father becomes a life-long memory of how the web of life at the pond connects us all.

Salmon Stream by Carol Reed-Jones, illustrated by Michael S. Maydak, follows the dramatic lives of salmon.

Over in the Ocean: in a Coral Reef by Marianne Berkes, illustrated by Jeanette Canyon. Stunning art accompanies delightful lyrics based on the classic tune of "Over in the Meadow."

Over in the Jungle: a Rainforest Rhyme by Marianne Berkes, illustrated by Jeanette Canyon. Similar to "Over in the Ocean," and irresistibly charming.

A Tree in the Ancient Forest by Carol Reed-Jones, illustrated by Christopher Canyon. The plants and animals around and under a grand old fir are remarkably connected to each other.

Earth Day Birthday by Pattie Schnetzler, illustrated by Chad Wallace. To the tune of "The Twelve Days of Christmas," this sing-along, read-along honors both the animals and the holiday.

THE AWARD-WINNING HABITAT SERIES by Anthony Fredericks, illustrated by Jennifer DiRubbio, features creature-communities, seen as part of their own unique neighborhood.

Under One Rock: Bugs, Slugs and other Ughs

In One Tidepool: Crabs, Snails and Salty Tails

Around One Cactus: Owls, Bats and Leaping Rats

Near One Cattail: Turtles, Logs and Leaping Frogs

On One Flower: Butterflies, Ticks and a few more Icks.

THE REMARKABLE UNIVERSE SERIES by Jennifer Morgan, illustrated by Dana Lynne Andersen, presents the amazing story of the Universe—explaining science in an exceedingly understandable and lively manner, narrated by . . . the Universe itself.

Born With a Bang: The Universe Tells Our Cosmic Story

From Lava to Life: The Universe Tells Our Earth Story

Mammals Who Morph: The Universe Tells Our Evolution Story

THE JOHN DENVER & KIDS SERIES by John Denver, in which Christopher Canyon adapts and illustrates some of Denver's best-loved songs in a heartwarming style that showcases Canyon's amazing abilities and brings a whole new dimension to these great songs.

Sunshine On My Shoulders

Ancient Rhymes: A Dolphin Lullaby

Take Me Home, Country Roads

Dawn Publications is dedicated to inspiring in children a deeper understanding and appreciation for all life on Earth. To review our titles or to order, please visit us at www.dawnpub.com, or call 800-545-7475.